Sammy the Shy Kitten

Sammy the Shy Kitten

by Holly Webb
Illustrated by Sophy Williams

tiger tales

For Daisy

tiger tales

5 River Road, Suite 128, Wilton, CT 06897
Published in the United States 2017
Originally published in Great Britain 2016
by Little Tiger Press
Text copyright © 2016 Holly Webb
Illustrations copyright © 2016 Sophy Williams
ISBN-13: 978-1-68010-401-1
ISBN-10: 1-68010-401-2
Printed in China
STP/1800/0168/1117
10 9 8 7 6 5 4 3 2

For more insight and activities, visit us at www.tigertalesbooks.com

Chapter One

"See you later, Mom!" Emma waved as her mom drove off down the bumpy road that led to Cloverview Stables. She was looking forward to seeing her best friend Keira, but she would see most of her riding-class friends at school on Monday. Really she wanted to say hello to the ponies, and the cats that lived at the stables, too.

Emma didn't always see the cats—they were all very shy, almost wild. She wasn't even sure how many of them there were; no one was. Liz, who owned the riding school, said she thought there were five. But Emma was almost certain there were six, and that the skinny orange cat was actually two skinny orange cats. Once she thought she'd seen him strolling along the roof of the feed store only seconds after he'd been sunbathing out by the paddock.

Liz put out food and water for the cats, but only once a day. Mostly they lived by hunting. They earned their keep by getting rid of the mice and rats that sniffed around the stables looking for the horses' feed.

"Hello, Sparky," Emma said, going

to pat the nose of the gray she usually rode in her class. The pony snorted and put his nose over the half-door of his stall. He nudged happily at her hand, searching for an apple or a carrot. He knew Emma always brought him treats. Emma giggled and brought out a piece of carrot. "And I've got mints for afterward, if you're good," she whispered. "But don't tell the others. I'll just go and let Liz know I'm here, then I'll be back to tack you up."

Emma looked around hopefully for the cats as she went over to find Liz, but none of them seemed to be around. She crouched down and peeked behind the tulips in the little flowerbed in front of the office. The orange cat (one of the orange cats, anyway) practically lived in the flowerbed, and sometimes he'd let her pet him. Sure enough, there he was, curled up tightly into a stripy ball. He opened one yellow-green eye and glared at her. He obviously didn't want to be petted.

Emma sighed and put her head around the office door.

"Hi, Liz. Mom dropped me off a little early so I could say hello to the ponies. I wanted to see if I could pet Midnight, too, but I can't find her."

Midnight was Emma's favorite of the stable cats—she was black and had longer fur than the others, with a thick bushy tail. She spent a lot of time lying in the sun and grooming, cleaning pieces of hay out of her pretty fur.

Liz had looked up, smiling, when she first spotted Emma, but now her smile faded. "I haven't actually seen her for a couple of days. I'm starting to get a little worried. I know the cats aren't really pets and they wander around all over the place, but usually Midnight's the friendliest of them all. She doesn't disappear like Coral and Candy, and she's almost always in the yard."

Emma nodded, frowning. "I don't think I've ever been to the stables and not seen her."

"She's been so hungry lately, but she hasn't come to the food bowls," Liz sighed. "I'm sure I'd have noticed her."

Emma glanced out at the bowls. Liz kept them by the bench in the yard, which had a wooden canopy built over it. It meant that the food stayed dry and the nervous cats didn't have to go inside for it. Emma smiled as she saw Susie, a thin little tabby, slinking over to see if there was anything left. But then she turned back toward Liz.

"So … Midnight hasn't eaten anything for two days?" she asked anxiously.

Liz shook her head. "Not from here, I don't think. She's a good mouser, so maybe she's just been hunting more. I wish I'd seen her around, though."

Emma nibbled her bottom lip. "At least the stables are far from the main road," she said slowly. Her Aunt Grace's cat, Whiskers, had been hit by a car a couple of years ago and had broken his leg really badly. He was better now, but Aunt Grace didn't like him going around to the front of the house. She always tried to tempt him back inside if she saw him sitting on the front wall.

Liz smiled at her. "Exactly. I'm probably worrying over nothing."

She didn't make Emma feel much

better, though. Where could Midnight have gone?

"Anyway," Liz said briskly. "We should get going. The others will be here by now." She got up and put an arm around Emma's shoulders. "Don't worry. You know what cats are like—especially these half-wild ones. We'll get all upset and then she'll stroll in without a care in the world."

Emma giggled. But she wished that Midnight would stroll in *now*.

Maybe it was because she was thinking about Midnight, or maybe it was just a bad day, but nothing seemed to go right for Emma that morning. Tacking up Sparky took forever. He wouldn't stay still—he jittered and sidestepped and nibbled at her jacket. Then he almost stepped on her foot as she led him over to the outdoor arena.

"Are you okay?" her friend Keira asked, as she finally managed to get to the gate. "You look a little stressed."

"Sparky's just being … Sparky," Emma sighed. "He's wonderful when he wants to be, but…."

Keira grinned and nodded. "I know. Maybe he's just excited."

"He's always excited!"

"Are you ready, girls?" Liz came over to check that their girths were tight. "Now, the jumps are a little higher than last week, but you're all perfectly capable of clearing these fences. Just don't let the ponies try to take them too fast."

Emma nodded a little nervously. She really did love Sparky. The gentler ponies, like Keira's mount Jasmine, just didn't have as much personality as the bouncy gray. But she had a feeling that trying to keep Sparky calm and collected wouldn't be that easy today. Luckily they were going first so Sparky wouldn't get bored. The thrill of riding a fast, eager pony took over as they set off, and Emma had a huge smile on her face by the time they'd cleared the second jump.

Then somehow everything went wrong. Maybe Sparky decided that he didn't like the look of the new rainbow-striped rails that Liz had used for the third jump. He slid around to the left of the jump instead of going over. Emma did her best to encourage him, but Sparky was determined—he swerved sideways around the jump, and Emma felt herself slipping out of the saddle. There was a horrible, slow moment when she knew she was falling. Then all of a sudden she was on the ground, with her ankle twisted and aching, and Sparky standing over her. He looked very apologetic.

"Emma!" Liz came hurrying over,

catching Sparky's reins and handing them to Keira. "Hold on to him, Keira, while I check that Emma's all right."

"I don't think I rode him at it straight enough," Emma said, wincing as she tried to stand. "Ow, my ankle…."

Liz gently felt the ankle through Emma's boot. "I don't think it's swelling up. Do you want me to call Alex and get him to bring you an ice pack?"

"It's okay. Sorry I messed up…."

"No, you were doing really well. It looked like Sparky just decided against that jump. Can you put any weight on your ankle?"

"I think so." Emma blinked, trying not to cry.

Liz helped her up. "Are you sure you're all right?"

Emma nodded. "It was just a shock…."

"Here, sit down on the bench. We'll tie Sparky up to the fence, and I'll come and check on you again in a little while."

Liz went back to schooling the others over the jumps, and Emma watched from the side of the arena, gently rubbing her ankle. It was starting to feel a little better already. She clapped as Keira jumped Jasmine clear, and her friend waved at her.

Emma stood up and leaned on the fence, testing the weight on her ankle. It was definitely feeling better. She was just thinking about asking Liz if it was okay to untie Sparky again when she heard a strange squeaky noise behind her. She glanced around. The outdoor arena was next to a shabby old barn that Liz was planning to get rid of, so they could make the arena bigger. It was divided up into stalls for horses, but they weren't used anymore. The noise was definitely coming from in there, though. Emma limped curiously over to the door—that was falling apart, too; a couple of the boards had rotted away at the bottom.

She lifted the latch, pushed open the door, and looked around it cautiously. Maybe a bird had gotten trapped inside—she didn't like the idea of it flapping out at her. But there was no bird, only the raspy creak of the door—and then that tiny, breathy little squeak again. Emma walked in slowly, following the noise. It sounded like it was coming from the stall at the end.

Emma stopped and peered around the open half-door. There was still some straw on the floor, piled up in the corner. The squeaking was coming from over there, and for one horrible moment Emma wondered if it was a rat.

Then a dark head looked up over the straw, and Emma laughed in surprise.

"Midnight!" she said, keeping her voice low. "Liz is really worried about you, you know. What are you doing in here?"

Midnight eyed her cautiously, her ears flickering, and Emma frowned. She'd never heard Midnight squeak like that before, she realized. And there was something else in the straw—something small and wriggly and dark. Actually there were several somethings....

"Oh! Midnight, did you...?" Emma stepped closer, trying to lean over the

20

door just a little so she could see without scaring the cat. She'd completely forgotten about her twisted ankle now. "You did! You had kittens!"

Chapter Two

The kittens were so sweet, squirming around over each other in the straw and nuzzling at their mother. Midnight glared suspiciously at Emma for a moment. Then she obviously decided that it was safe to ignore her and went back to licking her babies all over. Emma tried not to giggle. It looked as though Midnight was determined that they would be just as beautifully groomed as she was.

"So that's why you were really hungry. It's okay, Midnight. I won't come any closer." Emma hung onto the doorjamb, counting. "It's three, isn't it?" she whispered. "Two black kittens and one gray tabby. I should go and tell the others…." But she didn't want to leave just yet. The kittens were so little. Emma wondered when they'd been born.

"I'd better go and tell Liz," she said at last, slowly backing away. "Don't go anywhere, okay?" She had read about mother cats picking up their kittens in their mouths to move them if they thought they weren't safe. She hoped she hadn't scared Midnight into doing anything like that. But Midnight didn't look too worried. "I'll get Liz to find you some food, too," Emma added, her eyes widening. "Oh, Midnight, you must be starving!"

As soon as she was out of sight of Midnight, Emma twirled around and limped out of the barn as fast as she could.

Liz waved when she saw her and hurried over. "Emma! I just noticed that you'd disappeared. How's your ankle? It doesn't look like it's swollen."

Emma shook her head, grinning at Liz. "No, it feels a lot better now. And I found Midnight."

"Oh, that's great! Where was she? Is she all right?"

Emma giggled. "She's more than all right. You have to come and see!"

"I need to watch the others. Can you show me at the end of class?" Liz glanced between Emma and the rest of the girls, and Emma realized that of course she couldn't leave them riding without an instructor.

"It's okay. I don't think Midnight's going anywhere." Emma folded her arms and glanced back at the barn.

Liz sighed. "I hope this is worth all the suspense, Emma! Come on, you'd better catch up with the others. Sparky looks like he's feeling left out."

Sparky did seem to think that he'd been missing out. He brightened up as he saw Emma and jumped two clear rounds with her as soon as he was allowed back into the ring.

"You rascal!" Emma told him affectionately, as she patted his nose afterward. "You can have a treat— here. But I don't think you deserve it. Why didn't you do that the first time around, instead of tossing me off?" Sparky gobbled up the treat from her hand eagerly, and Emma smiled.

"I guess if I hadn't fallen, I wouldn't have found the kittens. Oh, look, Liz is waving. It's the end of the lesson now—I can't wait for her to see them." She hugged Sparky around the neck and started to walk him back to the gate where the others were waiting. "I'm not showing you, though. I wouldn't trust you not to put your huge, clumpy feet on those kittens."

"What are you so excited about?" Keira asked, as she led Jasmine over toward Emma and Sparky.

"I found Midnight! Liz hadn't seen her for a couple of days, and she was getting worried. You have to come and see!"

Keira looked at her doubtfully. "I'm sorry, Emma. You know I'm scared of cats."

"I forgot! I'm sorry, I was just so excited." She bit her lip, not wanting Keira to miss out on the secret. But she knew her friend was especially frightened of the half-wild cats at the stables. She leaned over to whisper in Keira's ear. "Midnight had kittens. In the old barn! Don't tell Liz, yet, okay?"

Keira smiled. "Now I understand why you're so excited. Are they cute?" She sounded a little wistful, as though she wished she wasn't so nervous around cats.

"I only saw them from a distance, but they were beautiful. Are you sure you don't want just a quick look?"

Keira shook her head. "Midnight's so jumpy…."

Liz came up behind them. "Are you going to show me this big secret now?"

Emma nodded eagerly, and Keira laughed. "She can't wait. I'm surprised she hasn't told everybody already! Here, I'll lead Sparky back."

Emma handed over the reins and hurried Liz along to the barn door. "Be really quiet!" she whispered, putting a finger up to her lips. Then she led the way inside, tiptoeing over the dusty floor.

"Where is she?" Liz whispered, and then she gasped as Emma pulled her sleeve and pointed into the stall. "Kittens! Oh, wow, I never even thought of that!"

"Three of them," Emma said, beaming. "Aren't they beautiful? Can we put some food for Midnight in here? I bet she's really hungry."

Liz nodded. "Yes, definitely. I'll go and get her some now. Gosh, three more cats. That's a lot…."

Emma looked up at her worriedly. "I hadn't thought about that."

Liz made a face. "Well, they are beautiful, but I'm not sure how many more cats we can take care of, to be honest. We've already got five. I suppose I should have expected this to happen, but none of them have had kittens until now. Probably we should have gotten them spayed or neutered, but they're all so shy. It was a nightmare the one time I had to take Coral to the vet because she'd been in a fight. She was really tricky to catch, and she hated being in the car."

"So...." Emma swallowed—her mouth had gone dry with excitement. When she spoke again, her voice sounded oddly squeaky. "If the kittens couldn't stay here, would you want to find homes for them?"

Liz nodded slowly. "That would be perfect, wouldn't it? Nice homes where they'd be taken care of and loved."

Emma gazed thoughtfully at the wriggling bundles of fur. "I didn't think of them being pets," she replied. "I thought they'd be a little wild, like Midnight."

Liz shook her head. "I think it has to do with how much they get used to people when they're little. Midnight and Susie and the others are half-wild because they've never had a real indoor home or spent much time around people. But it doesn't mean it has to be the same with these little ones."

Emma nodded. That made sense.

"How are you going to find homes for them?" she asked. "Would you just … ask people if they wanted them?"

Liz smiled at Emma. "I suppose so. Are you thinking you'd like a kitten? What would your mom and dad say?"

"I don't know." Emma sighed. "But I can ask. I love the idea of taming a little wild kitten!"

Liz snorted. "I wouldn't put it that way to your mom, Emma. She'd worry about you getting your fingers bitten off. Come on, let's go and find Midnight something to eat."

Chapter Three

"Dad!" Emma ran over to the car where her dad was waiting and flung her arms around his waist. "You'll never guess what happened!"

Her dad blinked at her in surprise. "Did Sparky behave himself for once?"

Emma shook her head and laughed. "Nope, actually he was really naughty, and I fell off. But I'm okay! It's

Midnight—she's had three kittens, and I found them!"

"That is exciting! Are they really small?"

"I think they're only a day or two old," Emma explained. "Liz said Midnight had disappeared for a couple of days, so I guess she went off to hide and make herself a little nest. The kittens are tiny—only about this big." She held her hands apart to show him. "Do you want to come and see?"

Dad wrinkled his nose. "I'd love to—but what about Midnight? Isn't she really shy? If a lot of people start trampling past her kittens, she might get upset."

Emma nodded. "I know. But Liz said that since I found them, I can take some food back for Midnight. You could come with me. Liz even made her a special treat—she found some fish in the freezer. She figures Midnight deserves it!"

Dad grinned. "I haven't seen any tiny kittens in years—not since my cat Bella had kittens when I was about your age."

"Did she?" Emma looked surprised. "Didn't you have her spayed, then?"

"She was a stray that Grandma May

adopted," Dad explained. "Well, she adopted us, really. She was sitting on the front doorstep one day when we came home from school. We hadn't even gotten as far as taking her to the vet, to be honest. We were just getting used to having a cat when the kittens arrived. We had her spayed after that…. One litter of kittens was fun, but your grandma didn't want to find homes for any more."

"You're so lucky," Emma sighed. "I wish we had kittens. Or a grown-up cat—I wouldn't mind." She gave her dad a sideways look. "Dad, if you really like cats, why don't we have one?"

Her dad looked thoughtful. "Well, it would have been tricky when Mom and I were both working full-time.

But I suppose now that we've changed our shifts around we could...." Emma's parents both worked at the local hospital. "I don't know what your mom would think, though, Ems. She's never had a cat."

"I don't see how anybody could not like a tiny little kitten," Emma said coaxingly.

"Maybe because it'll turn into a great big cat clawing the sofa? You know your mom likes everything really clean and neat in the house."

"A cat could be clean and neat...," Emma said hopefully. "Oh, look! Liz has the food!" Liz was standing by the parking lot gate, holding a couple of bowls. Emma grabbed her dad's arm, hauling him after her.

"We'll be really careful," she told Liz, as she took the food bowl. "Oh, you brought some water, too. I was going to ask you about that."

Emma's dad took the water bowl and followed Emma across the yard to the old barn. "I can hear them rustling around," he whispered to Emma as they tiptoed over to the stall.

Midnight was looking anxious, and she half stood up as Emma and her dad came to the door of the stall. The kittens squeaked a little and shifted around in the straw nest as their mother moved. Emma ducked her head, trying to see the kittens without staring at Midnight—she knew from a cat program she'd seen on TV that cats didn't like to make eye contact sometimes. "It's okay," she whispered. "We brought you some yummy food. Fish—can you smell it?"

She was sure that Midnight's whiskers flickered, and the fluffy cat was definitely eyeing the bowls.

"I'll put the food here." Emma crouched down and stretched out her arm, trying to get the bowl into the stall without scaring Midnight. "And Dad has some water for you, too." She glanced across at her dad.

"Can you see the kittens? Look, they don't even have their eyes open yet!"

The kittens wriggled and made tiny meowing noises, calling for Midnight to feed them. They were like little furry balloons, Emma thought, all plump and squishy. Their fur was still short and fine, so the pink skin showed through on their tummies and paws, and their tails were almost as thin as string.

"I wish we could stay and watch," she whispered to Dad as she edged away, still crouching. "But Midnight might not want to eat while we're here because it'll mean leaving the kittens."

"I know. She is looking a little worried," Dad agreed. "I love that little tabby. It looks like it's going to have beautiful silver and black stripes. But they're all cute."

"I like that one, too," Emma whispered, giving the kittens one last look from the doorway. "That's the kind of cat I've always imagined having."

Snuggled in the straw, the kittens meowed faintly, and stumbled their way over toward their mother and her milk. They were so little that food and warmth were the only things they understood. They heard the soft vibrations of Emma's voice, and her dad's, but only Midnight understood that Emma had brought food and water and had kept her distance from the precious kittens.

"The kitten of one of those cats at the stables?" Emma's mom asked doubtfully. "I don't think that's a very good idea, Emma. I know they look beautiful, but none of them is friendly. They're all half-wild. I don't think we want a cat like that." She put the salad on the kitchen table and sat down. "It isn't that I don't want us to have a pet, but we've never had a cat before.

Shouldn't it be somebody who really knows what they're doing taking care of kittens like those?"

"But there isn't anybody who knows!" Emma tried to argue. "Liz would be really happy if we wanted to adopt one. I know she would. You should see him, Mom, the little gray tabby kitten. He has white paws and white under his chin. His nose is all pink and soft because he's so small."

Mom smiled at her. "He sounds beautiful, Emma. But a kitten like that might be a lot of work. Maybe we could find one from somewhere else."

Emma looked desperately at her dad. She should be delighted—Mom had never said anything about being able to get a cat before. Emma knew that she was lucky to have her riding lessons—she'd never thought they'd be able to have a pet at home, too. But now she didn't want just any cat; she wanted to help those little kittens at the stables.

She'd always felt sorry for the stable cats, not having real homes to go to. They didn't seem to mind—they curled up together in the stalls, and Liz put food out for them—but it wasn't like a cozy, warm basket by the radiator, or sleeping at the foot of someone's bed. She didn't want the kittens to grow up wild like their mother, even though Midnight was beautiful.

"Let's see what we can find out about taming kittens," Dad suggested. "They *were* very sweet. And I think it's too late to turn Emma off of them. She's already fallen in love with the little tabby. Do you think it's a boy or a girl? We didn't get close enough to check."

"I thought he was a boy, just because he looked like he was wearing a little white shirt. But I don't know for sure."

Emma's dad looked over at her mom, and she smiled.

"We'll see," Mom said. "I'm not promising anything, but maybe you could do some research. Find out what we'd have to do...."

"Yes!" Emma squealed. "Oh, Mom, this is so exciting! Please can we hurry up and eat lunch so I can look it all up on the computer?"

"Hello, Cloverview Stables?"

"Hi, Liz," Emma said, a bit shyly. She'd never called the stables before. Usually Mom did it if they had to book a lesson.

"Oh! Is that you, Emma? Is everything okay? How's your ankle?"

"It doesn't hurt at all now. I'm just calling because I've been talking to Mom and Dad about the kittens. I asked if we could adopt one, but my mom's not sure. She says maybe it should be somebody who's more experienced with cats." Emma frowned to herself, trying to remember all the information that she and Dad had looked up that afternoon. "But the thing is, if they're going to be adopted, the kittens need to have lots of contact with people, so they're not shy around humans like Midnight and the others are. So I was wondering if I could come and spend some time with them."

"Yes, that makes sense," Liz said slowly. "And it's wonderful that you want to help take care of them, Emma. Of course you can, if your mom and dad are fine with it."

"Oh, they are," Emma told her. She hesitated, and then went on, "I'm really hoping Mom will let me adopt one of the kittens, if I can help tame them. At the moment she's worried that they'll be too wild. But we've found lots of ways to help with that. Dad and I have been doing a lot of research. It's the little tabby one I really love."

"He's adorable, isn't he? So, is there anything I should be doing? Or the others at the stables?" Liz asked.

"I think just try to spend some time with them. Would it be okay if I came to the stables after school sometimes, as well as for my lessons? The more the kittens get used to people, the better. I'm guessing you want to find homes for the others, too?"

Emma heard Liz sigh on the phone. "Yes, I need to think about that. Maybe I'll put a flyer up on the board outside the stables."

"Oh!" Emma suddenly remembered something she'd read on a website.

"There's a charity that will help with spaying and neutering the cats. They'll even come and get them for you! They'll catch them and neuter them for free, and then bring them back."

"Really? That sounds amazing. Could you find their details for me, please?" Liz laughed. "You really are serious about cats, aren't you, Emma?"

Chapter Four

Emma went to the stables whenever she could get Mom or Dad to drive her. She spent most of her allowance on a cat care book, just in case she did manage to persuade Mom to take the tabby kitten home. The kitten wouldn't be allowed to leave his mother until he was seven or eight weeks old, anyway. They had to give the kittens the chance to learn everything they needed to know from Midnight. So Emma had plenty of time to read the whole book *and* persuade her mom that the tabby kitten would be the perfect pet.

The first time she went, Emma just sat quietly by the door. Midnight watched her suspiciously, her ears laid back and the tip of her fluffy tail twitching. It was obvious to Emma that she was making Midnight nervous, but she had to get to know the kittens. It was so important. She wrapped her arms around her knees and just sat listening to the squeaks and rustles in the straw. By the time Dad came to pick her up, Midnight was lying down feeding the kittens as if Emma wasn't there.

On her next visit, Emma decided to bring Midnight some cat treats. If Midnight was distracted, she might let Emma near the kittens. Liz had told her that Midnight had licked the bowl of fish spotlessly clean, so Emma decided to get fish-flavored ones.

She crouched down a little ways away from the kittens and shook some treats out of the packet next to Midnight. The cat sniffed at them curiously. Emma could tell she wanted the fishy treats, but that she wasn't ready to eat in front of her. Emma sat with her chin on her knees, looking away from Midnight. Out of the corner of her eye, she could just see Midnight edging closer to the pile.

Midnight made one last little hop and started to gobble down the treats. Then she sniffed cautiously at Emma's right foot—the part of her that was closest—and darted back to her kittens. Emma couldn't stop herself from beaming. It felt like a breakthrough.

She opened the packet again, making sure that Midnight could hear it rustle. Then she wriggled a little closer, shaking out a few more treats right next to the cat. Emma really wanted to get a good look at the kittens, as she thought they must be just over a week old by now. She was hoping that their eyes would be open. Her cat book said that the kittens would all have blue eyes to begin with.

"They're definitely bigger," Emma whispered to Midnight, who was still eating the treats. "They're beautiful." Midnight looked up at Emma with her ears laid back, and Emma sighed. "I know you don't like me talking. I don't want to scare you. I just want them to get used to hearing my voice. Anybody's voice, really."

Midnight crunched the last fishy treat, and Emma took a deep breath. She had petted the cat a couple of times before, but not since she'd had the kittens. Slowly, she held out her hand to let Midnight sniff it.

Midnight nudged her nose at Emma's hand cautiously, but she didn't hiss or raise the fur on her back. She actually looked calm. She rubbed her chin along Emma's wrist, and then strolled back toward the kittens.

Emma held her breath and put the same hand down in the straw, next to the kittens. Midnight lay down, stretched out beside her babies, and Emma smiled delightedly. She was almost touching them! And the little tabby was right next to her hand. Emma wondered if he could smell the fishy treats, too, but she thought he was probably too young for that. His eyes were definitely open, though—just tiny blue slits. He looked like a teddy bear, with his round face and little triangle ears.

"I'm so lucky," Emma whispered, "getting to know you now when you're so small."

The kitten meowed squeakily and waved his front paws, wriggling closer to Emma. "I'm not your mom, little one," she whispered. "I think you want to be over there. For some milk." Very gently she scooped him closer to Midnight, so he could latch on and suckle. His fur was the softest thing she'd ever felt.

"I've got to think of a name," Emma muttered. "I can't just keep calling you little one. Sam maybe? Or Sammy…. You look like a Sammy. My little Sammy cat."

As the weeks went by, Sammy and the other kittens grew amazingly quickly. By four weeks they could all walk properly, and suddenly they seemed to be interested in everything.

Midnight spent a lot of her time trying to herd them back together, hurrying around them in the scattered straw and shooing them back to the nest. But as soon as she had one kitten safely tucked away, the other two would be padding out to explore again. Emma thought that Midnight looked very tired. Liz had been putting down a lot more food for her than usual, and Emma had been bringing her bowls of special cat milk and extra snacks, but it was hard work herding kittens and feeding them, too.

The kittens were more like mini cats now—their heads still seemed much too big for their little bodies, but they'd lost their furry balloon look. They were really growing up.

"Hello," Emma whispered, crouching down by the door of the stall. Three little heads popped up at once, and she giggled. They looked so funny, like the meerkats she'd seen at the zoo. Almost at once the tabby kitten plunged over the edge of the straw nest to come and see her.

"I've got something really special for you," Emma said. She and Liz had been talking about how they were going to wean the kittens—to get them eating food as well as Midnight's milk. Emma had looked it up in her book, and Mom had bought some baby rice and evaporated milk from the supermarket to mix up for the kittens. It looked disgusting, but then Emma didn't much like the look of regular cat food, either.

She'd bought a special litter box as well to put in the corner of the stall. According to her book, now that the kittens were trying solid food, they were going to poop a lot more, too. Until now Liz had just scooped out the dirty straw every day.

Liz had said that she'd be able to do

most of the feedings and cleaning, and Alex and Sarah, who also taught at the stables, had said they could help, too. The kittens were going to need to eat four times a day, so it was lucky Liz and the others were around.

"This is going to be yummy," Emma promised, dipping her finger in the white goo and holding it out to Sammy.

Sammy sniffed curiously, and Emma rubbed the goo on his nose. He stepped back in surprise and sneezed. Then he licked at the dribbles of baby rice that were running down his muzzle. It was good! He licked harder, running his bright pink tongue all around his mouth and nose.

Sammy padded closer to the girl, hoping for more of the white stuff. Emma was holding some out for him, and he licked it right off her finger this time, trying to gobble it up fast. He could hear his brother and sister coming up behind him, and he didn't want to share.

"Look," Emma whispered. "There's a whole bowlful…."

Sammy sniffed hopefully at the bowl, and then started to lap hurriedly. The other two kittens appeared beside him, and his sister plunged her face into the bowl eagerly. She came up smeared in white milky stuff, dripping from her nose and her black whiskers.

The girl laughed, and all the kittens jumped, staring at her nervously.

"I'm sorry," she whispered softly.

Sammy watched her for a moment, then decided that she didn't mean any harm and went back to lapping. The food was so tasty, but it was making him sleepy, just like feeding from his mother did sometimes. He licked at the last smears at the bottom of the bowl, and then licked his whiskers and yawned.

His brother and sister began to pad back toward their mother, to sleep curled up next to her, but the nest in the straw was a long way away. Sammy yawned again and eyed the girl. She was warm, too—he knew it from the times she'd petted him. He walked toward her, wobbling a little, and tried to climb up her leg.

Emma looked at him, smiling in delighted surprise. Then she gently scooped a hand underneath his bottom and lifted him up onto her lap. Sammy flopped down, full and sleepy, and began a tiny purr.

"Oh, Emma," Mom whispered from the doorway. "Is that Sammy? You said it was the tabby one you really liked."

"Yes," Emma breathed. "He fell asleep on me. And he was purring, Mom."

"He is beautiful," Mom said, smiling. "What does Midnight think about him sleeping on you?"

Emma giggled. "She's asleep, too. I think she's grateful! She must be worn out taking care of them all. I need to ask Liz if she has something we can put across the doorway of the stall, a plank of wood maybe. So that Midnight can get out, but the kittens won't. Otherwise they'll be wandering all over the place soon. We might never find them!" She sighed. "I guess we have to go, don't we?"

"We can stay for a little longer. I don't want to make you move him. Why don't I go and ask Liz about finding something for the door?"

Emma nodded. Then, as her mom was turning to leave, she suddenly whispered, "Mom!"

"What is it? Is he waking up after all?"

"No, it's just … do you think we could adopt him? You said we had to see about having one of Midnight's kittens—in case they were too wild."

Her mom looked down at Sammy, stretched out blissfully on Emma's knee. "He doesn't look very wild, does he?"

Emma shook her head, beaming.

Mom smiled at her. "All right, we can adopt him. I'll tell Liz now."

Chapter Five

Keira stood by the door of the stall, looking cautiously around it at Midnight and the dancing kittens. Emma had managed to persuade her to come and see them at last. They were playing with a toy that Emma had bought—a bundle of feathers on the end of a long wire that she could flick and wave around. The kittens loved it.

They stalked it, pounced on it, bounced around it, and all the while Midnight sat watching them proudly. Every so often she couldn't resist and put out a paw to dab at the feathers, too.

"They're so funny," Keira whispered to Emma. "I wish…."

"You could take a turn," Emma suggested, holding out the toy.

Keira shook her head. "No," she said quickly. "It's okay."

Emma wanted to persuade her, but she had a feeling it would only make Keira feel worse. "I want to wear Sammy out a little, before Dad comes and we put him in the cat carrier," she explained. Dad was bringing the carrier when he came to pick Emma up from her lesson, anytime now.

"Do you think Sammy won't like it?" Keira asked.

"I don't know." Emma sighed. "It feels mean taking him away from Midnight and the other kittens, but he's about nine weeks old. Lots of kittens go to new homes then, even though it's a little early. From the websites Dad and I looked at, it sounded like it'd be best to adopt Sammy as soon as possible. Otherwise, he'll do whatever his mom does. Midnight still doesn't really like being touched, and she'd never let me pick her up. I don't want Sammy to learn to be scared of people from her."

"What's going to happen to the other kittens?" Keira asked.

"Liz thinks she's found a lady who wants them," Emma said happily. "She's had cats before and she's going to take them both together. Later this week, I think." She glanced anxiously at Midnight, who was still watching her

71

kittens closely. "Poor Midnight. She'll really miss them. But it's the best thing for the kittens, I'm sure."

"Oh! Your dad's here," Keira said, turning to look out the barn door.

Emma let out an excited gasp. "Oh, wow...," she said. "I'm actually getting to take you home, Sammy!"

She had brought along a packet of cat treats, so they could tempt Sammy into the carrier. The kittens were eating dry food like Midnight now, although theirs was made for kittens. The cat treats were a special extra. Emma took the carrier from her dad and opened the wire door. Then she scattered a few treats inside. Midnight and all the kittens edged closer—they knew what that rustling noise meant.

"They're all coming," Emma said worriedly to Dad.

"That's probably not a bad thing. We want Sammy to think the box isn't scary. If they all play around in it for a while, he won't mind going in, will he?"

"I guess not." Emma watched as all three kittens explored their way around the carrier, nibbling at the treats and sniffing the soft cushion lining. Even Midnight snapped up a treat that was just by the door.

"Emma, look," Dad whispered, a few minutes later. "Sammy's going in on his own. You can close the door in a second."

Emma nodded, and as the white tip of Sammy's striped tail cleared the door, she gently swung it shut and twisted the latches.

"Let's go home," she whispered.

Sammy sat pressed against the back of the box. He had no idea what was happening—he'd never seen anything but the barn. Now he was shut into the small, shadowy carrier, and somehow it was moving. The smells were strange and sharp, and there was so much noise. The vibration of the car was completely new to Sammy and very frightening.

He could hear Emma's voice, and her dad's, and he knew that they were familiar, but it wasn't making him feel much better.

"Do you think he's all right? I thought he might meow, but he's not even making any noise."

"It's a big shock for him, poor kitten. We're almost home, Emma."

"We're almost home," Emma repeated, whispering through the holes in the carrier. "Not much longer."

Sammy felt himself pressed against the side of the carrier as the car swung around a corner. He let out a little hiss of fright and tried to back further into the box—but there wasn't anywhere to go. He scratched at the plastic, just a faint little movement of his paw. Nothing happened. Sammy closed his eyes and hoped his mother would come.

"I don't understand," Emma whispered. "He was so friendly before. He let me pick him up. He even slept on my lap."

"One of those websites did say to expect a kitten to take a couple of steps backward when it's moved, Ems," Dad pointed out. "He's only been here a few hours."

"I didn't think he'd be this jumpy." Mom looked worriedly at Sammy, tense and nervous, his whiskers bristling.

"He's just scared," Dad said encouragingly.

"I guess so…," Mom sighed.

Emma looked over at the big wire crate they'd borrowed from one of the neighbors, whose puppy didn't need it anymore. Sammy couldn't be loose in the house just yet, as he'd probably run off and hide. But they could put the crate on the table in the corner of the kitchen, and he could see everything that was going on and get used to lots of people being around. The kitchen didn't have any holes a kitten could get stuck in when they let him out to play.

It had seemed like the perfect plan for an almost-wild kitten. But Emma had imagined Sammy watching curiously as she ate her breakfast or did her homework. She'd thought of him purring to Dad as he made dinner. She hadn't seen a hissing, spitting, miserable little kitten hiding at the back of his crate. He'd even swiped at her with his claws when she put a bowl of fresh water in for him. He'd missed, but still. It was like Sammy was a different kitten.

"We need to give him time," Dad said gently. "A day or so to calm down, before we start trying to handle him again."

"Yes," Emma sighed. "And I know I should have expected that he wouldn't be very happy...." But she hadn't thought it would be like this. Mom looked so worried—and she'd really been warming up to the idea of a kitten!

What if she changed her mind?

Dad patted Emma's shoulder, and then gave Mom a hug. "Don't look so tragic, you two! It'll be okay! I'm going to make some coffee. Do you want anything, Emma?"

Emma shook her head. Deep down, she realized sadly, she'd just thought that Sammy would see how nice their house was. He'd know how excited she was to have a kitten of her own—he'd understand, and he'd settle in right away.

"I was being silly," Emma muttered to herself. She crouched down in front of the crate, looking at Sammy sideways. He was still huddled in the back, his ears flat against his little head. "I thought everything would be perfect all at once. But I'll do anything to make you love us, Sammy. I just want you to be happy."

Chapter Six

Emma held out her fingers to Sammy. They were covered in roast chicken dinner baby food, which apparently was the most popular flavor with kittens. It felt sticky and gloppy, but she didn't mind. They'd given Sammy an entire 24 hours to calm down, and Emma just couldn't wait anymore. All the websites said that the way to make a half-wild kitten like you was to use food. They had to make Sammy see that food came from people, and if he wanted the food he had to put up with them, too.

"He's noticed, Ems," Dad breathed behind her. "He can smell it."

It was true. Emma could see Sammy's ears flickering, just a little. And his eyes were widening. "He must be able to smell it," she said. "It smells *disgusting*."

"Not to a cat," Dad whispered back.

"He's coming!" Emma tried not to sound too excited, or too loud. Sammy was stepping delicately, cautiously across the crate to sniff at her fingers. His tiny pink tongue flicked out, and he began to lick them.

Emma held her face straight, trying not

to laugh and scare him away, but it tickled so much. His tongue was very strong for such a small kitten. And it was so rough. Emma leaned a little closer, so she could see the tiny white hairs all over his tongue. Sammy stopped licking and glanced worriedly up at her for a second. But then the deliciousness of the baby food won, and he went back to getting every last bit out from under Emma's fingernails.

Emma wanted to pull her hand away to get some more from the jar, but she was sure that would frighten Sammy. Then she rolled her eyes. Of course! She dipped her other hand in, lifting out several fingerfuls, and slowly moved that hand into the crate, too.

Sammy moved his head from side to side, as though he wasn't sure which hand to go for.

"Aww, poor Sammy—you've confused him now," Dad said.

Sammy decided that he couldn't get much more from Emma's right hand and changed to gulping down the food from her left. Emma looked at him thoughtfully. Her right hand was still in the crate. Very gently, she ran her hand down Sammy's back. He tensed a little, but he didn't spring away. Emma kept softly petting his fur.

"Is that nice?" she whispered. "Is it nice being petted?"

Sammy glanced up at her, as if to check what the noise was, but he kept licking.

"Keep petting him," Dad whispered. "I'm going to get a little bowl of his dry food. Let's see if we can get him to eat that with us still here watching him."

He filled the bowl quietly and passed it to Emma so she could put it in front of Sammy. The little kitten darted back as the bowl suddenly appeared, but then he caught the scent of the dry cat food he was used to. He gave Emma's fingers one last hopeful swipe with his tongue and moved on to the bowl.

"You try petting him," Emma whispered to Dad.

Dad nodded and reached slowly into the crate, running one finger down Sammy's back as he busily gobbled the food. Sammy glanced over his shoulder, but he didn't stop eating.

"It really works," Dad said. "We can do this again when we feed him at lunchtime."

Emma nodded. "Every time we feed him. And maybe soon we can get him out of the crate and let him eat from his bowl on the floor." She sighed happily. "It's really going to be okay, Dad. I'm sure it is."

"Which top do you think I should wear?" Mom held two out on hangers.

"Hmm. The black one," Emma said, watching Sammy. He had almost finished his bowl of food and was looking sleepy. She had her arm inside his cage, with her hand cupped around him. Emma had a feeling he might fall asleep with her hand still there, which would be wonderful. He'd be almost back to the same friendly Sammy she'd known at the stables, and it was only a week since they'd brought him home.

"Are you sure?" Mom frowned. "You didn't look for very long…."

"Yes, Mom. I can pet Sammy *and* look, you know. Hurry up! Aunt Grace will be here to babysit soon."

Mom rushed off, and Emma giggled and gently moved the food bowl. Sammy had fallen asleep with his head in it! He twitched a little and then flopped down, collapsing across her hand with a little wheezy snore. She leaned against the crate, closing her eyes and smiling dreamily to herself. Soon they'd be able to take him out of there and he'd be a real pet. She was sure of it.

"Are you asleep, Emma?"

"Oh! Aunt Grace. I'm not, but Sammy is." Emma reached out the arm that wasn't in the crate to hug her aunt. "I didn't hear you come in."

"Your dad was walking up the path when I pulled up, so I didn't have to ring the bell. He just went to change his clothes. So this is Sammy? He's beautiful."

"Isn't he?" Emma agreed proudly. "And he's getting much more confident again. He was really upset on Saturday when we brought him home, but he's a lot happier now." Carefully, she slid her hand out from underneath him, and Sammy snuffled but stayed asleep. She grinned at her aunt. "My arm feels all prickly now! Mom asked if you could please help me with my science homework, and then she got a DVD for us to watch afterward."

Emma yawned and snuggled against Aunt Grace. "Can't we watch a little more?"

"No! You know your mom said eight thirty, young lady. Besides, don't you have to feed Sammy before bed?"

"Oh, yes, and you haven't seen him awake yet! I forgot!" Emma sprang up from the sofa. "I'll go and get his food." She hurried into the kitchen and began to measure it out, while Sammy padded up and down the crate, watching her and meowing hopefully.

Emma had just opened the door of

the crate to put the bowl in when Aunt Grace pushed open the kitchen door. It banged slightly, and Sammy jumped at the noise. He saw Aunt Grace—someone he'd never met before—and suddenly panicked. He hissed loudly, and Emma stared at him. "What's the matter, Sammy?"

"Oh, dear, is he okay?" Aunt Grace asked, leaning over to look at him.

Sammy hissed again as he saw the strange person coming closer. He darted out of the crate door, desperate to get away.

"I think he's a little scared because you're new," Emma said worriedly, trying to catch him. "Maybe you'd better just let me calm him down, Aunt Grace."

Aunt Grace stepped back out of the kitchen, but Sammy was already spooked. He scrambled over Emma's arm in a panic, accidentally clawing at her wrist so that she squeaked and dropped the food bowl.

The bowl smashed on the tiles with a huge crash, and Sammy yowled in fright. He raced around the side of the crate, but the table was pushed up against the wall below the window and there was nowhere to go. Frantically, he clawed his way up the curtains, digging his tiny claws into the fabric.

Sammy hung there, swaying a little. He didn't really understand what had happened. He'd been about to eat his food—he could smell it—and then suddenly everything was different and terrifying. Now he didn't even know where he was, or how he'd gotten so high up.

The curtain fabric ripped a little under his weight, and he slid down a few inches with a frightened meow. He tried to claw his way back up again, but the shiny fabric was difficult to climb, and he slipped further down.

"Sammy, it's all right...." Emma's voice, low and soothing. And now he wasn't falling anymore. Her hands were around him, the way they were when she fed him sometimes. After struggling for a moment, he let her unhook his paws from the few last threads of the curtains, and sat tensely in her hands, ears back and fur fluffed up. She lifted him down, still whispering gently, and slid him back into the crate. Sammy backed away from the door anxiously, but the strange person was gone now, he could see. It was just Emma. He knew her. She was safe.

Chapter Seven

"Emma! You're still up!"

Emma jerked awake. Mom was standing in the living-room doorway, looking surprised.

"I'm sorry," said Aunt Grace. "Emma was upset, and I didn't want to make her go to bed…."

"What happened?" Dad asked, just at the same time as Mom noticed Emma's scratched wrist and swooped down to check it.

"Emma, you've hurt yourself! Oh, no, was it Sammy?"

"He didn't mean to." Emma looked sleepily at Dad and Mom. "It was an accident. And, um, I broke his food bowl. I'm sorry.... We swept it up."

"What's been going on?" Dad sat down on the arm of the sofa, and Mom came to sit next to Emma.

Emma sighed. She was so tired that it was hard to explain. "I went to feed him, but he was scared of Aunt Grace."

"It was my fault. I should have thought, of course, he's never seen me before," Aunt Grace put in. "And he's more nervous than most kittens. I frightened him and he jumped out of the crate and scratched Emma by accident."

"And that made me drop his bowl, and he got even more scared and ran up the curtains."

"Oh my goodness," Mom muttered.

"I'm afraid he did tear them a little," Aunt Grace went on slowly. "But he's back in the crate now and he's calmed down. In fact, the last time Emma checked, he was asleep, wasn't he?"

Emma nodded.

Mom leaned back against the sofa and let out a huge sigh. "I knew this was a mistake. We should never have brought him home. He was so upset when we took him away from the stables and his mom. I just don't think it's fair."

"Mom!" Emma gasped.

"Oh, Emma. You have to see I'm right—just look at your wrist!"

Emma looked down at the three long red lines, and the little scratches that she'd gotten all over her hands when she was taking Sammy off the curtains. They were sore, but it hadn't been Sammy's fault. He was just scared— he hadn't meant to hurt her.

Mom put her arm around Emma. "I know how hard you've tried with Sammy, but he might not be the right cat for us after all. He needs to go to a shelter, I think. Where they've got people who are used to taking care of cats like him."

"I'm not sure," Dad said. "I know Sammy was difficult when we brought him home, but he is getting better."

"Getting better!" Mom stared at him. "Emma is covered in scratches!"

"I don't think it's that big of a deal," Aunt Grace said gently. "Even Whiskers scratches me sometimes if I go to pick him up and he just doesn't feel like it."

Mom sighed again. "I'm sorry, Emma, but he's too unpredictable. I'm not sure he's ever going to be really friendly. Maybe he needs a home more like the stables, where he doesn't have to be around people if he doesn't want to."

"Mom, please don't send him away!" Emma wailed. "I don't want any other cat, only Sammy! He'll be fine, I know he will. I'll do anything to keep him." She stared pleadingly at her mom, tears trickling down her cheeks. She couldn't bear the thought of poor Sammy going to a shelter—somewhere else strange and new and frightening. He'd have to start all over again, and soon it would be too late to tame him. He'd be shy and wild forever.

"Just give us a few more weeks, honey," Dad suggested. "Of course today's a little bit of a setback, but we have to keep trying."

"Two more weeks." Mom looked from Emma to Dad and back again. "We should be able to tell by then, shouldn't we?"

Dad nodded slowly. "All right. Emma?"

"I guess so," Emma whispered huskily. She was so upset that her voice seemed to have disappeared. Two weeks! It was no time at all.

"What's the matter?" Keira asked, as she led Jasmine past Emma and Sparky. "Is Sparky being a pain about getting tacked up again? You look, well, a little sad...," she trailed off, not sure what to say. Emma looked like she might be about to cry.

"No." Emma sniffed. "Actually Sparky's been great. Maybe he can tell I just can't deal with a mischievous pony today."

"Oh, no! What is it?" Keira swapped Jasmine's reins to her other hand and gave Emma a hug. "Don't cry!"

"I can't help it." Emma's voice shook. "Mom says we might have to give Sammy to a shelter. She thinks we can't handle him."

"But wasn't it going really well?" Keira said, confused. "You showed me that photo your dad took of him eating off your fingers. He looked so happy."

"He's still jumpy, though," Emma gulped. "Mom thinks he's not going to adapt to living in a house. He got scared last night because my aunt was there and he scratched me. I didn't mind—not much—but Mom was really upset about it. She says we have two weeks to prove he can be a pet, or he has to go." She was crying so much that she could hardly get the last words out.

Keira hugged her tighter, and even Sparky and Jasmine leaned in close, as if they wanted to make Emma feel better.

"Two weeks is a long time," Keira said. "Honestly, it really is. And I saw how friendly and tame he was with you here. You almost had *me* petting him, Emma, and I'm scared of cats!"

"I guess so…," Emma said, between gasps. "It doesn't feel like long, though. If he goes to a shelter he'll be all lost and alone. It'll be awful."

"Then you absolutely have to make sure it doesn't happen," Keira said firmly. "I'll see if I can think of anything to help." She gave Emma one last hug. "Ems, we have to go. Liz is waving at us. She wants us to try those dressage aids today, remember?"

Emma nodded and sniffed hard. "I'm okay. I'm so glad I told you about it, Keira. I do actually feel a little happier."

Emma grabbed her riding hat from the back seat and looked anxiously at Aunt Grace's purple car parked outside their house.

"It's all right," Dad said soothingly. "She said she wouldn't go near Sammy. Although we will have to try and get him used to meeting new people eventually. She has something for you."

Emma hurried down the path, curious to see what Aunt Grace had brought. She had a feeling it was something important—not just a magazine or some chocolate to cheer her up, but something that really mattered.

"Emma! I'm so glad you got back before I had to go to work. Look, I brought you this." Aunt Grace whirled out of the front door onto the path. "Here. I really hope it helps."

Emma looked down at the book that her aunt had pressed into her hands—*Taming Feral Kittens*. There was a sweet little orange kitten on the front of it, with a shy, worried look on its face that made Emma think of Sammy at once.

"I got it at the animal shelter. I thought I'd go and ask them if they had any tips for you. They were so friendly and helpful. This was written by someone who used to work there, and they said to call if you get really stuck. I wrote the number inside the cover for you." She hugged Emma. "Sweetheart, if Sammy does have to go there, they will take good care of him, I promise."

Emma nodded. "But it's not going to happen," she said firmly. "This is terrific, Aunt Grace. Thank you! I'm going to go and read it now."

Sammy sat in the doorway of the crate, looking out suspiciously. Everything was different—the crate had been moved down onto the floor, and he didn't like that, for a start. He preferred to be high up, so he could see who was coming. High up was safe.

But he liked the open door. He thought he did, anyway. He sniffed the air beyond the crate, his whiskers twitching. He could step out, right onto the floor. He could explore. Cautiously, he extended one paw over the door frame, and then the next, and then his two back paws.

He stood nervously just outside the crate, watching, scanning the room. Emma was there, sitting in the corner, and her dad was over by the counter. She wasn't looking at him—she was gazing off into the distance as if she hadn't noticed what he was doing. Sammy took a few steps out into the room and sniffed.

Food! He could definitely smell food. He was sure it was well past his usual feeding time. He'd been expecting Emma to bring food, but instead she and her dad had put his crate down onto the floor. Determinedly, he stomped across the floor toward the smell. Emma had his bowl on her lap. He stopped a few steps away from her, looking uncertainly at the bowl. He wasn't sure he wanted to go any closer, but he was hungry.

His tail swished from side to side, and then he made a panicked little run, flinging himself at the bowl. What if she took it away? Sammy climbed up on Emma's leg and started to gobble down the food as quickly as he could.

"It's all right," Emma whispered. "I'm not going anywhere."

Sammy's ears flickered, but he didn't stop eating. Then he felt her petting him, very gently running her hand over his shoulders and down his back. It was nice—it felt like his mother licking him. He slowed his eating down a little, almost sure that the bowl wasn't going to be taken away.

At last, he'd finished the entire bowl. He licked around it carefully and then sniffed it to make sure there wasn't any more. There wasn't, but he was full anyway.

Slowly, carefully, he settled down into a crouch on Emma's lap. She was still

petting him, so gently. Sammy stretched
out his paws and kneaded them up and
down on Emma's skirt. Then he closed
his eyes and purred.

Chapter Eight

Emma tucked the phone under her chin so she could talk to Aunt Grace and have both hands free for scrambling after the ping-pong ball as Sammy sent it skittering around all over the floor.

"It really works," she told her aunt, a little breathlessly. "We started on Sunday after I'd had time to read the book. All this week, we've only fed him with the bowl on me or Dad, so that he has to come to us to get his food. And he's always hungry, so it works perfectly. The very first time we tried it, he let me pet him and he even purred! I'm starting to think he actually does like me," she added shyly.

"Of course he does. Oh, that's wonderful, Emma! I felt awful when your mom said you might have to give him up."

"Me, too. But I'm hoping she's going to let me keep him. She was laughing at him this morning when he was playing with his feathery toy before school. He was trying to catch it so hard that he kept almost falling over backward." Emma threw the ping-pong ball again for Sammy. "We're doing the next thing it says in the book now. He's going to be allowed out in the kitchen all the time, not just for food time and playing. His bed and his litter box are still in the crate, but we'll leave it open so he can come and go when he wants to."

"And then I suppose you'll bring his bed out, and eventually get rid of the crate?"

"Exactly. I don't know how long it's going to take, though. The book says it depends on the kitten. Oh, Sammy!"

"What did he do?" Aunt Grace laughed at the other end of the line.

"He chased after the ball so fast that he ran into the cupboard. He's fine; he just looks a little confused. Hold on just a minute." Emma laid the phone on the floor and wriggled closer to Sammy, whispering comforting noises. She was sure that he looked embarrassed, if a kitten could. His ears had gone flat.

"It's okay," she whispered and without thinking about it, she scooped Sammy gently into her hands and snuggled him up against her sweater. "Oh… I didn't mean to…." It was the first time she'd ever picked him up. But Sammy hadn't clawed her, or jumped away in fright. He was huddled against her, so tiny and fragile that she could feel his heart beating under her fingers. "You don't mind?" she said. "Oh, Sammy, I do love you…."

"Hey…," Dad whispered from the doorway. "He looks happy!"

"Dad, can you pick up the phone?" Emma whispered. "I was talking to

Aunt Grace. She must be wondering what happened to me. Can you please tell her I'll call her later?"

Dad chuckled. "Sure. I'll tell her you're occupied with some very important business."

"Are you sure?" Emma looked worriedly at Keira. "I mean, I'd love it if you came over for lunch. But I know how you feel about cats."

"Exactly," Keira called back, as she hefted Jasmine's saddle over to the tackroom. "And so does your mom. So if even silly Keira isn't scared of playing with Sammy, he must be okay as a pet, right? The two weeks are up, aren't they? We need to show your mom how good Sammy is."

"Two weeks yesterday. I haven't wanted to ask Mom what's happening." Emma sighed. "And I never said you were silly," she added quickly.

Keira grinned. "I know. But I am silly.

I can't even say what it is that makes me frightened of cats. They just make me so nervous."

"I don't want you to be miserable." Emma frowned. "And…." She nibbled her bottom lip. "If you're nervous, it might make Sammy nervous, too," she explained. "He was all right with Aunt Grace when she came over during the week. She was really good. She just sat on the floor completely still until he was brave enough to sniff at her. But she's used to cats, and she wasn't scared."

"I won't be scared, either," Keira said. "I promise. I said I'd try to think of something I could do to help, and this is it. I'll be brave." She smiled at Emma. "Honestly. I'll be fine."

"He's in here, in the kitchen." Emma looked back at Keira. She could see her mom hovering behind her friend with an anxious expression on her face. Mom obviously wasn't sure about this—neither was Emma, to be honest. But Keira seemed so certain. She'd explained to Emma's mom in the car that she wanted to try and stop being scared of cats, and that she knew she'd be okay with Sammy because he was so little.

Emma opened the door slowly and peered around. "Oh, he's asleep in his basket. Actually, that's good. How about we sit on the floor for a while? We can have a snack, and then when he wakes up we can let him come and see you."

Keira nodded. Emma thought she looked pale. But she looked determined, too. "That's a good idea."

Emma took her hand, pulling her gently into the kitchen to sit down half under the table. That would give Sammy plenty of space to get a good look at them before he got out of his basket. Keira even giggled when Emma's mom handed them a plate of cheese cubes and apple to eat under there. "It's like being really small and making tents under the table. Did you ever do that?" she whispered.

"Yes! Hey, I think he's waking up." Emma glanced at her. "Sure you're all right?"

"Mmm-hmm."

Emma could feel Keira tensing up beside her. Maybe it *was* a bad idea, after all. But it was too late to do anything about it now.

Sammy stretched and yawned, and popped his head up out of his basket to see what was happening. He was hungry and he could smell something delicious. Not his regular food, but that only made it more exciting. He twitched his ears forward and gazed at Emma under the table. Emma and someone else. He flicked his tail from side to side worriedly. It wasn't someone he knew, but she was sitting very still. She had some of whatever it was that smelled so nice; he could see it in her hands. And she was holding it very close to the floor....

Sammy hopped out of his basket and set off across the floor, his whiskers trembling as he smelled the cheese. He nudged his head against Emma's feet on the way, as if to say that she belonged to him. But he was still more interested in the cheese. He padded between Emma's legs and the new girl's, and sniffed hopefully at the girl's fingers. She was holding that piece of cheese as if she didn't really want it at all.

He froze for a second, ears flickering, expecting someone to shoo him away. But no one did. Swiftly, Sammy grabbed the scrap out of her hand and gulped it down, savoring every crumb.

Then he licked Keira's fingers, just to check that he hadn't missed any. He felt her laugh—her fingers shook—but there was no more cheese. He gave her one last lick and turned to scramble up into Emma's lap. He could still smell cheese, and he was sure that if Emma had any, she'd give it to him. He hauled himself up her leggings, breathing hard, and half fell into her lap. Then he sat there and gave a massive yawn, showing all his tiny sharp teeth and his raspberry-pink tongue.

"He's beautiful," Keira whispered, sounding surprised.

"You didn't mind when he licked you?" Emma asked. She couldn't stop smiling—Sammy had perched himself on her lap like he belonged.

Keira wrinkled her nose. "Actually, I was really scared. But he's so little— I just kept thinking I could run out if I couldn't deal with it."

"Oh, Keira," Emma's mom whispered. "Do you want to go into the other room?"

Keira shook her head. "No, I think it's okay," she said cautiously. "He's really good."

Emma's mom nodded. "I guess he is." She smiled at Emma. "So, are you having lunch under the table, then?"

"I don't think we'd actually get much of our lunch if we did that." Slowly, carefully, Emma moved onto her knees, cuddling Sammy against her fleece top as she stood up and went to sit on one of the kitchen chairs. She was waiting for him to leap away, but Sammy only stretched his neck out so he could peer over the edge of the table at the plate of sandwiches that her mom was putting down.

Keira laughed. "He's eyeing the food as though you never feed him, Emma."

"He can't think he's making a habit of sitting on your lap at mealtimes," Mom said sternly. "Just this once."

Emma stared at her delightedly. "You mean...."

Her mom nodded. "Yes—I was talking to your dad about it last night. Sammy's so much happier now. Oh, Emma, watch out! He's going for that ham sandwich!" She quickly pulled the plate back, and Sammy looked disappointed.

"I'll get you some in a minute," Emma whispered in his ear. "A whole sandwich, if you like!"

Sammy yawned again and purred a little and rubbed his face against her hand. Then he nuzzled at Emma's top, and pawed his way gently over the zipper, snuggling down inside.

Emma looked down lovingly at the little tabby kitten curled up inside her fleece. "Sammy, you're staying!"